For Betty-Jean,

our kids,

and grandkids.

CONTENTS

RUSS THOMPSON

ALL ALONE

Finding Forward

Books

Published by Finding Forward Books. P.O. Box 8182, Long Beach, CA 90808. www.findingforwardbooks.com.

Editing by Laura Perkins. Series concept by Pam Sheppard. Text set in Open Dyslexic Mono.

ISBN: 979-8-7469368-2-0 (Amazon paperback)
ISBN: 978-1-7373157-2-8 (Ingram paperback)
FILE: FF004-14M-20240606

Summary: Tenth-grader Elgin Hobbs is caught in a downward spiral. He's failing classes, his divorced parents fight, and his mom is an alcoholic. Life keeps bringing him down. But he fights to rise above it.

BISAC Subject Codes: YOUNG ADULT FICTION / Family / Marriage and Divorce | YOUNG ADULT FICTION / Social Themes / Drugs, Alcohol, and Substance Abuse | YOUNG ADULT FICTION / Social Themes / Self-Esteem and Self-Reliance

Lexile Readability Measure: HL-540-L

1 FIFTEEN NOW

SUNDAY AFTERNOON. I wait at the top of the stairs outside our apartment.

It's cold out here. But I hate being around Mom when she's drunk.

Dad pulls up to the curb. I walk down the stairs and get in his car.

Then it happens.

Mom runs down the stairs and sticks her head in his window.

"Where's my money?" she screams. "I need the child support."

"Get back," Dad says. "I came to pick up Elgin."

"You're not leaving," Mom says. "I need my money! Now!"

Dad inches the car forward.

Mom screams. "I want my money!"

Dad speeds up. Mom runs beside the car.

He goes faster. She falls. Dad slams on the brakes.

I jump out and run back to Mom. Dad kneels next to her.

"Gina, are you okay?" he asks.

Pop! Mom socks Dad in the face. Blood spurts out of his nose.

He swings his arm back to slap her.

"Stop!" I yell.

Dad drops his arm.

I lift Mom and help her walk up the stairs to our apartment.

I set her on the couch. She flops over sideways and falls asleep with her mouth open.

I'm fifteen now.

I'm not a kid anymore.

But I'm crying like one.

2 CAN'T TAKE IT

MONDAY MORNING. It's still dark. My clock says five-thirty.

I used to be okay with sleeping on the couch. But the mattress is worn out now. It makes my back sore.

I listen as Mom moves around in the kitchen.

She was drunk all day yesterday. I wonder if she remembers what happened with Dad.

I listen as she steps into the living room. I bury my face in the pillow and keep my eyes closed.

She bends down and kisses me on the cheek. "I love you," she says.

I pretend to sleep.

The front door opens and closes. I listen to her footsteps as she walks down the stairs.

I don't know why I didn't answer her.

ONE HOUR LATER. I get out of bed, get dressed, and fold up the couch.

I go to the kitchen. There's no milk in the refrigerator.

I knew there wouldn't be.

I eat dry corn flakes for breakfast and drink the last of the orange juice.

I need to make lunch. But there's no peanut butter, no jelly, and no cheese slices.

I put two pieces of bread

together with ketchup between them.

At least it will look like a sandwich when I eat lunch with Shane.

Whatever Mom makes as a waitress, there's always enough for her to drink.

Whatever Dad makes at his warehouse job, there's always enough for him to gamble.

Everything else comes last.

EDISON HIGH SCHOOL. I walk through the front gate.

Shane stands by the tenth-grade lockers.

"Elgin, how was it with your dad yesterday?" he asks.

"I didn't get to go with him."

"What happened?"

"It's a long story."

We've been friends since third grade. But there are some things I just don't talk about.

MATH. Mr. Braden comes to the front of the classroom.

"Some of you have been sitting here and not paying attention," he says. "We're going to try something new today."

He holds up a big plastic jar with cards in it.

"I wrote your names on cards that I put in this jar," he says. "From now on, I'm going to draw names to call on you. You won't be raising your hands."

This is bad. I'm terrible in math.

Mr. Braden reaches in the name jar, pulls a card out, and points to the board.

"Lexie, could you read the first problem?" he asks.

She begins reading. "On a trip from Boston to Philadelphia, Mr. Smith drives 309 miles and uses 11.4 gallons of gas. How many gallons will he use if he drives 140 miles from Philadelphia to Washington, D.C.?"

She's one of the smart ones. I wish I could read like her.

"You get five minutes," Mr. Braden says. "Get to work."

I copy the problem onto my paper. But I have no clue what to do.

I look sideways. Shane moves his arm to let me copy.

I don't understand the answer. But at least I can put something on my paper.

Five minutes pass. Mr. Braden comes to the front. He pulls a name out of the jar.

I feel my face sweat.

"Elgin, could you come up and solve the problem?" he asks.

I don't get up. Everybody looks at me.

"Elgin, could you come up?"

I stand, put on my jacket, and walk out the door.

I know I'll get in trouble.

But I just can't take it.

3   MAKE THINGS WORSE

TUESDAY MORNING. I walk through the front gate. School starts in twenty minutes.

I feel like a freak. My pants are too short.

I pull them lower. I'll be pulling them lower all day.

Shane opens his locker. "Mr. Braden was mad when you walked out of class yesterday," he says.

"I couldn't take it anymore."

"You know you're in trouble."

"I know. But I did what I did."

MATH. Mr. Braden gives me his mad look when I walk through the door.

I try to act like I don't care.

"Elgin, where did you go yesterday?" he asks.

"I needed to get out."

The bell rings. He gets on the security phone.

"Room twenty-four," he says. "Pick up for the guidance room."

The security guard, Mr. Dirzo, comes to the classroom. He's an old guy who looks like a grandpa.

Some people call him Mr. Dirtso behind his back. But I don't. I like him.

Mr. Braden gives him the referral. We go into the hall.

"Elgin, what did you do this time?" Mr. Dirzo asks.

"I had to get out. I just

couldn't take it."

"Was that the right thing to do,
to walk out of class?"

"No. But I just couldn't take
it."

GUIDANCE ROOM. Mr. Wiley waves me
into his office.

He's strict. But he's always
straight with me.

"Elgin, you keep messing up," he
says. "What's going on?"

"Mr. Braden is calling on
everybody now. I just don't like
being called on."

"Is that the right way to make
something better, to run away?"

"No. But I just didn't want him
to call on me."

"Are you doing your homework?"

"Sometimes."

"Is that the best you can do?"

"No."

He gets on his computer and frowns. I wonder if he's looking at my grades.

"The reality is that you have to change," Mr. Wiley says. "You're smart. But you're lazy. And you need to think about what you're doing. I'm giving you three detentions."

It's no big deal. I've done detention lots of times.

"How are things at home?" Mr. Wiley asks.

I put my head down. "Still bad. Still the same."

"I know it's been tough for you," he says. "But you have to let the bad stuff go. You can't let it bring you down."

I like Mr. Wiley. But he doesn't

know what it's like.

It's not as easy to change as he thinks it is.

ART. We sit at our tables and do pencil drawings of an old tennis shoe.

Ms. Somoza looks over my shoulder.

"Elgin," she says. "Good job on the laces. The shading is excellent."

That's what I like about her. She always has something nice to say.

I'm getting an A in this class. It makes me wonder if I could be an artist someday.

HISTORY. Mr. Rubio comes to the front of the classroom.

He's a good teacher. But he's

strict. You can't say anything unless you raise your hand, and he calls on you.

I drop my pencil. It rolls under Lexie's desk.

"Could you get that?" I whisper to her.

"Elgin, no talking," Mr. Rubio says. "You have one detention."

"But I was asking for my pencil."

"You just talked back. That's your second detention."

"How am I supposed to do my work if I don't have a pencil?"

"You now have three," Mr. Rubio says. "Do you want more?"

I feel like telling him to shut up. But I think about Mr. Wiley and don't say anything.

It will only make things worse.

4 RATHER BE COLD

TUESDAY AFTERNOON. School's out. I walk with the crowd to the front gate.

Everybody smiles and laughs. They're glad to go home.

But not me. I hate going home.

I keep hoping Mom will quit drinking. But it never happens.

Lexie walks ahead of me. I wish I could be smart like her.

She looks like a normal person with her dirty shoes and faded uniform pants.

But she's smart inside. She always knows the answers.

Our grades come out on School View tonight. She'll probably get all A's.

Not me. I might be getting four NoPasses.

HOME. I walk up the stairs and open the front door.

The alcohol smell hits me as soon as I come in.

I go to the kitchen. Mom stands at the sink, rinsing out her coffee cup.

She has that numb look on her face. She's drunk.

"Elgin, I got a call from Mr. Wiley," she says. "He told me you ran out of your math class. I also got a call from Mr. Rubio. He said you talked back to him."

Her speech is slurred. I wish I could leave. But there's no place to go.

"I also got in trouble from my boss for talking on my cell phone when they called," she says. "Who do you think you are?"

There's nothing I can say.

Her hand flies up.

I take the slap and look back at her like it was nothing. I don't want her to know it hurt.

"You keep messing up," she says. "It needs to stop."

She's right. It needs to stop.

I wish her drinking would stop.

EVENING. I'm still hungry. The child support still hasn't come.

We had watered-down soup for

dinner.

It wasn't enough.

I sit at the kitchen table with the laptop open. Mom is in her room.

She's probably drinking from the bottle she keeps in her closet.

I finish my homework in English and history.

It's not very good. But it's done.

I go to the school website and click on math.

It's another word problem like the one we had in class.

I can read the words. But I can't understand what it's about.

I write down some numbers to make it look like I tried.

That's all I can do.

I get on School View. Report card grades should be online by now.

I don't want to look.

But I have to.

I have an A in art and a C in PE.
But I have NoPasses in math,
science, English, and history.

Four NoPasses.

I stare at the screen. The grades
don't change.

I've never done this bad before.

TEN O'CLOCK. I lie in bed. I can't
sleep.

Then I remember.

I grab my pants for tomorrow, get
Mom's sewing kit, and go to the
kitchen table.

She told me not to do it. But I'm
tired of listening to her.

I measure the legs with a ruler,
cut off the bottoms, and sew hems to
make them into shorts.

I know it's going to be cold
tomorrow.

But I'd rather be cold than
laughed at.

5 WONDER HOW MUCH

SUNDAY AFTERNOON. I sit at the bottom of the stairs, not the top like I did last Sunday.

When Dad gets here, I can jump in his car quicker. We can get away before Mom comes down the stairs.

I look at the street where they fought last week.

Mr. Wiley said I have to forget about the bad stuff.

I wish I could.

Dad pulls up. I run to his car and jump in the front seat. He pulls away before Mom comes down.

I'm so glad there was no drama.

"Elgin, how was your week?" Dad
asks.

I think about my grades and how
bad I felt when I saw them.

"Everything was fine," I say.
"Where are we going today?"

"Price Mart," he says. "You need
school pants. We can also get you
some new shoes."

I know I should have told Dad
about my grades.

But I want this to be a nice day.

PRICE MART. We go to the section
where they have school uniforms.

I find the pants I need, navy
blue. I'm surprised when Dad gets me
three pairs.

Next, we go to the shoe section.

Dad gets me Price Mart shoes.

I wish I could get better ones. But at least they don't have holes in them.

We go to the check-out counter. Dad puts his credit card into the machine.

It beeps.

"Let me try again," Dad says to the check-out lady.

It beeps again.

He tries again.

It beeps again.

We leave my stuff behind and hurry to the parking lot.

Dad's face is bright red. I know not to say anything.

We get in the car. Dad stomps on the gas when we reach the street.

I didn't do anything wrong. But I feel like I did.

DAD'S PLACE. We walk up the stairs
to his apartment.

I'm glad he's calm now. He's
probably thinking about the football
game.

We go in the front door. Francine
comes out of the kitchen and gives
me a big hug.

"Elgin, I'm so glad to see you!"
she says.

She's nice. But I never hug her
back. I don't know why.

"How come you don't have any
bags?" she asks Dad. "I thought you
were going to Price Mart."

"We have to go back," Dad says.
"The bank messed up on my credit
card."

He sits on the couch and turns on
the football game. Francine sits
next to him.

His laptop is on the coffee table. He opens it and begins typing.

"Yes!" he says.

"What happened?" Francine asks.

"My credit card is fixed now. We can go back to Price Mart after the game."

He gets up and goes to the kitchen. I look at the computer screen. It's a gambling site.

I guess he won.

In the fall, it's football. In the winter, it's basketball. In the spring and summer, it's car races.

It's not the sports that he cares about. It's the gambling.

I hope it's true that we'll go to Price Mart after the game.

Maybe we can also get pizza.

EVENING. Dad drops me off in front of our apartment.

It turned out to be a nice day.

Mom and Dad didn't fight. My new shoes aren't so bad. I got three pairs of pants. And we went out for pizza.

I unlock the front door. The living room is empty.

I look in Mom's room. The alcohol smell hits me. She's asleep on top of her bed.

Everything is bad again.

I wonder how much she drank today.

6 REGULAR PERSON

MONDAY MORNING. PHYSICAL EDUCATION.
We finish the half-mile run and come
back to the roll-call area.

I know what's coming next. I wish
it wasn't.

"The test today is push-ups," Mr.
Quinty says. "When I call your name,
come to the front. Keep your back
straight. Lower yourself until your
elbows bend ninety degrees. Push
yourself all the way up."

He gets down in front of us and
does five perfect push-ups. I bet he

34

could do fifty.

"Alex Ortiz, you're first," Mr. Quinty says.

Alex comes to the front and does thirty-one push-ups. He makes it look easy.

I don't want it to be my turn.

"Lexie Franklin, you're next," Mr. Quinty says.

She comes to the front and does twelve push-ups. The girls clap for her.

"Excellent," Mr. Quinty says. "Elgin Hobbs, your turn."

I go to the front. Everybody looks at me. It's going to be bad.

The first push-up is okay. The second one is harder.

On the third, my arms start to shake. By the fourth, I barely make it to the top.

I try to do a fifth. But I can only get halfway up.

"Good effort," Mr. Quinty says. "Carlos Davila, you're next."

I watch as everyone else does their push-ups.

Every guy and half of the girls do more than me. Even Lexie is stronger than me.

I try to act like it doesn't matter. But it does.

"I've said it before," Mr. Quinty says. "You can all improve. But this class isn't enough. You have to do extra to get better."

I have to do something. Maybe I'll try.

LUNCH. My new shoes feel better on my feet now. It's cold today, so it's also nice to have new pants.

I sit with Shane at our table in the food court.

The child support came, so I have a real sandwich today. I made peanut butter and jelly.

"You ready for your tryouts?" I ask Shane.

"I hope so," he says. "I worked on my shots all weekend. There are a lot of good guys going out."

We used to be the same height. But I stayed short, while Shane got tall.

He's a good basketball player now. I think he can make the team.

"How was it with your dad yesterday?" Shane asks.

"It was cool," I say. "He took me shopping. Then we watched the Jacksonville game."

I never tell Shane about how it

really is.

I always look forward to seeing
Dad on Sundays.

But when I'm with him, I feel
like I'm in the way.

It's like he doesn't want me
there.

HOME. I open the front door and hear
coughing.

Mom sits at the kitchen table
with her coffee cup.

I smell the alcohol on her
breath.

"What happened?" I ask.

"I had to leave work because I
was coughing too much. But I'm
starting to feel better now."

She looks worn down and tired.
Her eyes are yellowish.

"Here's money for dinner," she

says. "Could you get me the usual?"

I leave the apartment for Burger House. It worries me that Mom is sick.

She's also drinking more.

BURGER HOUSE. I order from the counter and sit at a table by the window.

It's busy tonight, with families and kids.

A man in white comes out of the kitchen and begins wiping tables.

He looks familiar from the back. I see his face from the side.

It's my history teacher, Mr. Rubio. He doesn't notice me.

I watch as he works, wiping the tables hard to really clean them.

"Mr. Rubio!" I call out.

He turns and sees me.

"Elgin, what's up?"

He smiles and comes to my table. His name tag says he's the manager.

"I didn't know you worked here," I say.

"They transferred me from the Burger House in Jasper."

"You work two jobs?"

"I started with Burger House when I was in high school," he says. "It paid my way through college. My wife and I are saving to buy a house."

"How often do you work here?" I ask.

"Three nights a week."

"You must get tired."

"Sometimes it's hard," he says. "But the extra money helps. You should apply here when you get older."

A worker comes up and says

something in his ear.

"Gotta go," Mr. Rubio says. "See you tomorrow."

I've never seen this side of him before.

He's like a regular person.

7 CAN'T QUIT

TUESDAY MORNING. SCIENCE. Ms. Acosta hands back our tests from yesterday.

Mine is another NoPass. I knew it would be.

She comes to the front of the classroom.

"There was a question yesterday about the best way to learn science," she says. "It's something that's easy and hard at the same time."

Here comes one of her speeches. I get tired of them.

"The key to everything is reading," Ms. Acosta says. "For example, I used to be a slow reader. All my classes were hard for me."

"My teacher told me to start reading everything twice," she says. "First, I started doing it in science. Then I started doing it in all my classes."

"It took more time at first to read everything twice," she says. "But my reading got better. My grades went up. And I went to college."

She makes it sound easy.

But I don't have time to read things twice.

HISTORY. Mr. Rubio hands back our tests from yesterday.

Most of the others smile when

they get their papers back. Lexie gets an A.

Mine is a NoPass. I thought I would at least get a D.

"Elgin, see me after class," Mr. Rubio says.

I go back and sit next to his desk when the bell rings.

"What's going on?" he asks. "I know you can do better than this."

I look away. I feel like I let him down.

"Did you study?" he asks.

"I tried to."

"What's that supposed to mean?"

I want to tell him. But I don't think he'll understand.

"You remind me of how I used to be," Mr. Rubio says. "I went through a lot of problems, too."

How does he know about my

problems? I've never said anything.

"I was in the ninth grade," he says. "My Mom ran off. I was alone with my dad. Things got bad."

"How do you mean?"

"He was doing meth," Mr. Rubio says. "He messed up in his job and got fired."

Mr. Rubio has always seemed perfect to me. How can he be saying these things?

"My dad started cooking and selling meth," Mr. Rubio says. "He got arrested and sentenced to six years. I had to live with foster parents."

I think about Mom. Once she starts drinking, she can't stop.

"I was failing in school. I felt like quitting. My foster dad said I had to forget about the bad stuff and not let it pull me down."

I think about Dad and how he gambles all the time. He cares about gambling more than me.

"I started doing my work in school," Mr. Rubio says. "My grades came up. I graduated and went to Jasper Community College. Then I went to Raymond State. That's how I got to be a teacher."

Maybe I can do better. I sit up higher in my seat.

"No matter what happens, you have to rise above it," Mr. Rubio says. "You have to forget about the problems, focus on your goals, and get your work done."

Mr. Wiley said the same thing. I'll try to work harder.

But I can't quit worrying about Mom.

8 EVERY DAY

WEDNESDAY MORNING. Shane is by the front gate when I get to school.

He stands in a group with some other guys who went out for basketball.

They talk and laugh. Shane doesn't see me when I walk by.

I guess he made the team.

LUNCH. I get to our table. Shane isn't there. I begin eating my sandwich.

Five minutes later, I'm still

alone.

I hear laughing and joking at the other end of the food court.

It's Shane and the basketball guys. I guess he has a new place to eat lunch now.

I don't want people to see me eating alone.

I get up and walk to the library.

AFTER DINNER. I sit at the kitchen table and turn on the laptop.

We're having a test tomorrow in science.

I read the chapter again. But none of it sinks in.

I remember when Mom and Dad still loved each other. Everything was good.

One day I was helping Dad wash the car. Mom came out to help. Dad squirted her with the hose.

Mom grabbed the bucket and dumped water on him. They laughed and chased around the yard.

But another time they were fighting.

Dad took Mom's vodka bottle and told her to quit drinking. Mom grabbed his arm and tried to take it from him.

Dad smashed it on the kitchen counter. They didn't care that I was watching.

I remember when Dad left us. I didn't think it would be forever.

But it was.

Mom is in her room now with the door closed. She said she was exhausted.

But she's probably drinking.

Mr. Wiley and Mr. Rubio told me

to forget about the bad stuff.

How can I do that when I'm right in the middle of it?

TWO HOURS LATER. I finish studying for science.

I've read everything twice again. I've never worked this hard for a test before.

Next, it's time for my arms.

I get on the floor and do four push-ups. They're hard.

I rest for a minute and do three more. Still hard.

I'm tired of being at the bottom.

I'm going to read everything twice and start studying.

I'm also going to start doing push-ups.

9 COURAGE

THURSDAY MORNING. I get out of bed and do four push-ups.

They feel pretty good. I rest and do four again. Then I do three.

They're easier than they were last night. Maybe I'm starting to get stronger.

I go to the kitchen and pour a bowl of cereal.

It's Mom's day off. Usually, she wakes up to eat with me.

But her bedroom door is closed. I wonder if she drank herself to sleep

Last night.

I finish eating and get ready for school. Mom's door is still closed by the time I have to leave.

I feel like knocking to say goodbye.

But she probably wouldn't hear me, anyway.

SCIENCE. I try not to be nervous about the test today.

Ms. Acosta comes to the front of the classroom.

"Take out your books," she says. "You get ten minutes to study."

I open my book and begin reading. I still remember what I studied last night. It's a good feeling.

Ms. Acosta passes out the tests. I know the first answer, the second, and almost everything after that.

It's the best I've ever done on a science test.

Maybe I can get a B.

PHYSICAL EDUCATION. It's Thursday, our day to run the mile.

Mr. Quinty leads us to the starting line.

"Do your best to run the whole way," he says. "Don't walk unless you have to."

It's four laps around the track. I've never run it all the way. Today, I'm going to try.

"Get ready," Mr. Quinty says. "Go."

At first, I keep up with the others. Then, they begin passing me.

I usually walk a few steps when I get tired. But not today. I keep running and finish the first lap.

"Elgin," Mr. Quinty says. "Two minutes and eighteen seconds."

I begin the second lap. It's hard to breathe. I want to walk. But I keep running.

Mr. Quinty calls out my time. "Four minutes and thirty-two seconds."

I begin the third lap. The muscles in my legs burn.

A guy in front of me slows down and starts walking. It feels good to pass him.

Mr. Quinty calls out my time. "Seven minutes and thirteen seconds."

One more lap. My lungs burn. I don't think I can make it. Another person quits in front of me.

I see the finish line. A hundred feet. Fifty feet. Ten feet. I'm done.

"Elgin, nine minutes and forty-two seconds," Mr. Quinty says. "Good job."

It's the first time I've ever gone a whole mile without walking.

I'm out of breath. My legs can barely move.

But I feel good about what I did.

LUNCH. I get to the food court and look for Shane.

He's not at our table. I see him sitting with the basketball guys. I guess that's his group now.

I don't want to eat by myself, so I walk to the library.

None of the books look good to me. Then I see one about a guy who was wounded in the army.

Both of his legs were blown off.

Now, he's a counselor for other soldiers who were in the war.

The picture on the front shows him playing wheelchair basketball.

The picture on the back shows him smiling.

I look at my own legs. I was able to run a mile today.

My problems are nothing compared to his.

I sit down and begin reading. It's a lot to think about.

10 GOING TO TRY

FRIDAY MORNING. MATH. Mr. Braden comes to the front of the classroom.

He points to the board. "Who wants to solve the first problem?"

Five people raise their hands. He calls on Lexie.

She goes to the front and reads the problem. "Alex needs 1.2 gallons of paint to cover a room that measures 9 feet wide, 11 feet long, and 8 feet high. How many gallons will he need to cover a room that measures 12 feet wide, 18 feet long, and 8 feet high? If paint costs $31.99 per gallon, how much will it cost to paint both rooms?"

I watch as she finds the answer. I wish I was smart, like her.

"Any questions?" Mr. Braden asks.

I'm lost. But there's no way I would put up my hand and show everybody how stupid I am.

"Remember the importance of math," Mr. Braden says. "You have to get a good grade in algebra. And you need it to get into college."

He says that every day. But I'll never be good in math.

And I already know I'm not going to college.

PHYSICAL EDUCATION. We finish playing soccer and line up outside the gym.

Mr. Quinty gives us each a paper with a list of exercises.

"A lot of you are improving," he says. "Some of you did better in the mile yesterday than you've ever done."

He looks at me and nods. I feel good for being noticed. He's never done that before.

"For those of you who want to do extra, I'm giving you these exercises to do at home. They take about twenty minutes. After you finish each day, have your parent sign at the bottom. You'll get ten points of extra credit each time you do the exercises."

I look at the list. It has push-ups, crunches, planks, lunges, and jump ropes.

"It's November now," Mr. Quinty

says. "Think about where you want to be in June. If you do these exercises every day, you'll be faster and stronger by the end of the school year."

Maybe he's right.

Maybe I'll try.

EVENING. I sit at the kitchen table. My homework is done. It took me a long time. But I did it right.

I also finished the extra-credit exercises for PE.

I need Mom's signature for Mr. Quinty.

The door to her room is closed. I knock. No answer.

I knock again. Still no answer.

I turn the doorknob and look inside.

Mom lies face down on top of the

bed. She moves a little but doesn't wake up.

There's a spot of blood on the side of her mouth.

There's a bottle of vodka on the nightstand.

I love her.

It scares me.

I don't know what to do.

NINE O'CLOCK. The house is quiet. Mom is still asleep.

I read the back cover again of the book I got from the library.

The guy in the book served with the U.S. Army in Iraq.

He was driving a truck when a roadside bomb exploded. He was the only one in the truck who survived.

He's trying to put his life back together. But he doesn't know if he can do it.

That's how it is for me.

Mr. Rubio said I have to work hard.

He told me to forget about my parents' problems and not let them pull me down.

My grades are bad. But I can bring them up if I study and do my homework.

I'm not good in PE. But I can get better if I do the exercises Mr. Quinty gave me.

I know what I have to do.

But I don't know if I can do it.

11 KNOW I SHOULDN'T

SUNDAY AFTERNOON. I sit at the bottom of the stairs outside our apartment. Dad should be here any minute.

Mom sits next to me. I know it's going to be bad.

"Elgin, don't worry," she says. "I just want to talk to him. It will only be a minute."

I wish I could believe her. But I don't.

Five minutes pass. Dad pulls up to the curb. I get in the front seat and hope for the best.

Mom goes to Dad's side. I'm glad his window is up.

"Where's my child support?" Mom screams.

Dad says nothing and looks straight ahead.

Mom bangs on the window with her fist. "I want my money!"

Dad says nothing.

Mom screams again. "I need my money!"

I get out of the car, walk across the street, and turn left.

If I go to Red's, I have enough money to buy a cheese pizza.

It will be quiet there.

THREE O'CLOCK. I leave Red's and text Mom to say I'm walking to Dad's place.

Thirty minutes later, I knock on his door.

I thought he would be glad to see me. But I can tell by the look on his face that he doesn't want me there.

Francine gives me her usual hug. We go to the living room.

"It's Carolina and Jacksonville," Dad says. "We can get something to eat when it's over."

He sits on the couch with his laptop open. Francine sits next to him.

When the game is on, Dad's eyes stay glued to the TV.

When a commercial comes on, he looks at his gambling site.

I feel like I'm not even there.

One hour later, Jacksonville scores a touchdown and wins. Dad and

Francine jump up and cheer.

They don't care about the game. It's the money.

I wonder if Dad used the child-support money to bet with.

EVENING. Dad drops me off. I walk up the stairs.

Mom gets up from the couch and hugs me when I come in the door.

Something is different.

I thought I would smell alcohol on her breath.

But there's nothing.

I look around.

The apartment is clean. The kitchen has been scrubbed.

"Elgin, how was it at your dad's?" Mom asks.

"Same as usual," I say. "We watched football."

"Did you talk?"

"No."

We go to the kitchen. Mom brings a plate of oatmeal cookies to the table.

She hasn't baked in a long time.

"I did some thinking and made some changes," she says. "Things are going to get better."

I finish my cookies and get up to throw the napkin away.

I see three empty bottles of vodka in the trash.

Maybe she's serious this time.

Maybe she's really going to quit.

TEN O'CLOCK. I sit at the kitchen table. It feels good to get my homework done.

Then I remember. My history report is due tomorrow. I have to write about World War One.

I don't have time to do it the
right way.

I get on the laptop, find a
website, and begin.

I only copy some of the words,
not all of them.

It's almost eleven when I finish.

I promised Mr. Rubio I wouldn't
miss any more assignments.

I know I shouldn't copy. But it's
late.

I won't do it again.

12 RIGHT THIS TIME

MONDAY MORNING. School starts in fifteen minutes.

I enter the front gate and go to my locker.

The more I think about my history report, the more I'm not sure.

I remember when Mr. Rubio talked about honesty.

He told us never to copy, that it's a form of lying.

I don't want him to think I'm a liar.

LUNCH. I go to the library, take out my history report, and read it again.

I wish I hadn't copied. But it's too late now.

Mr. Rubio probably won't notice. It's better to turn in something than nothing.

HISTORY. Mr. Rubio comes to the front of the classroom.

"Read your reports one more time," he says. "Make any final corrections that are needed."

I look at my report. I don't feel good that it's copied.

"Time's up," Mr. Rubio says. "Pass up your papers."

This is it. I have to make a decision. I keep my report instead of turning it in.

THE BELL RINGS. Everybody leaves the classroom.

I go back to Mr. Rubio's desk.

"Elgin, what's up?" he asks.

"I didn't turn in my report."

"I thought I saw it in your hand," he says. "What happened?"

"Parts of it were copied."

He frowns. Maybe I shouldn't have told him.

"I'm glad you're telling me," he says. "But why did you copy?"

"I forgot about it until late last night."

"It shows me a lot that you're being honest now," he says. "Why did you change your mind and decide not to turn it in?"

"I remembered what you said about telling the truth. I was trying to do right."

"Can I see the report?"

I give it to him and watch his eyes as he reads it.

"I can tell it's copied," he says. "Your grade would have been a NoPass."

I'm glad I decided to be honest.

"Do you keep a list of assignments and due dates?" he asks.

"No."

"Start doing it," he says. "And never mess with your integrity again. Whenever you lie, sooner or later the truth comes out. You will not be trusted in the future."

I never thought of it that way. I'm glad I told the truth.

EVENING. I sit at the kitchen table, doing homework.

Mom is in her room already. She

said she was tired from work.

I hope it's true. I hope she's not drinking.

I try to study for math. We're having a test tomorrow. But I can't figure out the word problems.

I wish I could talk to Mr. Braden. But I know he doesn't like me.

History is next. I have to rewrite the report I copied. I look up three different articles, make an outline, and begin writing.

It's not as hard as I thought it would be.

I will only get partial credit. But I feel good about doing it right this time.

13 GOOD TIRED

TUESDAY MORNING. MATH. Mr. Braden passes out the tests.

"Keep your eyes on your own papers," he says. "Check your answers when you finish. Good luck."

The first section has fifteen number-problems. I think I can do most of them.

But the second section has two word-problems. I look at the first one.

If Mr. Jones needs 1.5 gallons of paint to coat a fence that is 90 feet long and 6 feet high, how many gallons will he need to coat a fence that is 60 feet long and 7 feet high? If the price of paint is $32.98 per gallon, how much will it cost him to paint both fences?

We had a problem like this in class last week. I couldn't do it then. And I can't do it now. The next problem is just as bad.

I go back and do the number problems. But I can't do the word problems.

Mr. Braden collects the papers.

"If you need help, remember that I'm here during lunch," he says.

Maybe I'll go. I have to do something.

PHYSICAL EDUCATION. We finish running the half-mile and sit on the grass.

I'm not as tired as I was yesterday. And I improved my time by four seconds.

Mr. Quinty stands in front of us. "We're looking for more people to join the Edison Eagles," he says. "It will get you in shape. And we do it in a fun way. It will also help you if you want to join the track team this spring."

I don't want to go out for track. There's no way I could be good enough.

But maybe I'll try the Edison Eagles. Maybe Mr. Quinty is right.

LUNCH. Mr. Braden's door is open. I'm nervous when I go inside. Three other students are also there.

"Elgin, good to see you," Mr. Braden says.

His voice is friendly, not like it is during class.

I sit in the front, next to the others.

"The Khan Academy is something that can really help you," Mr. Braden says. "I'm thinking about using it for the entire class. Look at the screen."

A man with a calm voice shows how to solve a word problem like the one we had on the test today.

It makes sense the way he explains it. I think I understand how to do it.

"I'm going to start matching the

lessons I teach in class to the lessons on the Khan Academy," Mr. Braden says. "If you do this lesson tonight, it will help you for class tomorrow. You can do the lessons as many times as you need if you don't understand them the first time."

I'll try it when I get home from school today.

Maybe the Khan Academy will help me.

AFTER SCHOOL. EDISON EAGLES. I put on my PE clothes and go out to the track with about thirty others.

I feel like I don't belong here. Everybody else seems stronger and faster than me.

"I'm glad to see all of you out here," Mr. Quinty says. "You'll be

working on your speed and strength.
You will also do some fun things. I
think you'll like it."

He numbers us off and puts us
into five teams.

First, we do stretching, jumping
jacks, and push-ups.

I'm surprised when I do five
push-ups.

Next, we run a half mile and the
fifty-yard dash. For strength, we do
lunges and more push-ups.

I'm tired when we're done. But
it's a good tired.

14 FIRST TIME

WEDNESDAY MORNING. MATH. I read the
warm-up assignment.

*Mr. Jones decides to spread grass
seed over his lawns to make them
greener. He needs 4.6 pounds of seed
for his front lawn, which measures
50 by 20 feet. How much seed will he
need for his back lawn, which
measures 45 by 40 feet?*

It's like the word problem I had
on the Khan Academy last night. This

time, I know how to do it.

I get to work. Five minutes later, I finish and raise my hand.

Mr. Braden looks surprised. I've never raised my hand to give an answer before.

"Elgin, come up and show us," he says.

My heart pounds when I walk to the board. I know I have the right answer. But what if I mess up?

I work out the problem and explain how I solved it.

Everybody looks surprised.

"Nice job," Mr. Braden says. "I knew you could do it."

He gives me a high-five. I feel good about what I did.

Maybe I can bring up my math grade on the next report card.

LUNCH. I look around the food court for someone I know.

Carlos and Marvin, two guys from the Edison Eagles, wave for me to sit with them.

It's nice that somebody wants me to join them, especially from the Eagles.

"How did you like the Eagles yesterday?" Marvin asks me.

"It was okay."

"This is our second year," Carlos says. "We joined because we were the slowest ones in our PE class."

"I got faster," Marvin says. "But Carlos is still the slowest."

"That's true," Carlos says. "But I'm the champion."

"Champion of what?" I ask.

"The slowest," Carlos says. "A few of us run the fifty-yard dash every week. The winner is the loser. And the loser is the winner."

"I won last week," Marvin says. "So, I was the loser."

"And I lost last week," Carlos says. "So, I was the winner."

I don't know what they're talking about.

But it feels good to laugh with them.

EDISON EAGLES. We sit on the grass by the track. Carlos and Marvin sit next to me.

Mr. Quinty stands in front of us.

"Whenever you do extra, you make yourself better," he says. "For example, all of you are making yourself better by coming out for the Edison Eagles today."

He looks at me and nods. I feel

good for being here.

"Life is not just what happens to you," Mr. Quinty says. "Life is about the choices you make. You all made the choice to be out here today. All of you who stick with it are going to make yourself faster and stronger."

We line up to do stretching. Everybody else is stronger and faster than me.

But I know I can get better.

AFTER DINNER. I open the laptop to read my history assignment. We're still on World War One.

At first, it's boring and hard to understand.

But when I read the chapter a second time, it seems interesting.

Our assignment is to answer

questions one through five.

I answer three of them without looking back at the chapter.

I've never been able to do that before.

I thought it would take me longer to do my homework because of reading the chapter twice.

But it didn't take as long as I thought it would.

Ms. Acosta was right when she said to read everything a second time.

I look at my list of homework assignments.

Everything for tomorrow is done.

For the first time in a long time, I feel good about school.

15 CAN'T STOP

FOUR MONTHS LATER. MATH. The bell
rings. Mr. Braden comes to the front
of the classroom.

"Open your books to page 263," he
says. "Who can do the first
problem?"

It's about an airliner, jet fuel,
and airspeed. I raise my hand with
about ten others.

Mr. Braden calls on Lexie. She
goes to the board. But she gets it
wrong.

I've never seen her miss a

problem before.

"Good effort," Mr. Braden says. "Elgin, could you come up and give it a try?"

I go to the front, write the equation, and draw the graph to go with it.

"Nice job," Mr. Braden says. "You did it perfectly."

I walk back to my desk. Lexie smiles when I pass her.

"Way to go," she whispers.

I try to keep a straight face and act like it's no big deal.

But it is.

AFTER SCHOOL. Track practice starts. We have a meet next week against Franklin.

We line up on the grass for exercises. I do twenty push-ups.

They're easy. I remember when I could only do four.

Mr. Quinty stands in front of us. He's going to give one of his speeches.

"Life is not easy," he says. "There are a million ways to fail. But you all have the ability to be successful."

He stops talking and looks at each of us.

"It's all about your attitude," he says. "It's about being determined that you will keep trying, no matter what, until you find a way to succeed."

Some people don't care what he says. But every time Mr. Quinty talks to us, it makes me want to try harder.

We go to the starting line. Today

we run the 1600 meters. It's four laps around the track, almost the same as a mile.

My best time is seven minutes and seven seconds.

I'm still the slowest guy out here, except for the shot-putters.

My goal is to break seven minutes.

"Ready, go," Mr. Quinty says.

I begin running. My legs and arms feel loose. I finish the first lap.

"One minute and forty-two seconds," Mr. Quinty says.

My breathing feels easy. I need to keep this pace. I finish the second lap.

"Three minutes and twenty-eight seconds," Mr. Quinty says.

I'm still on a pace to break seven minutes.

The third lap is harder. I keep
running.

"Five minutes and eighteen
seconds," Mr. Quinty says.

One more lap. I have to move
faster. I'm behind the pace I need
to break seven minutes.

I round the first turn. I can't
get enough air.

I round the second turn. My mind
goes blank.

Fifty yards. Twenty-five yards.
Fifteen yards. I cross the finish
line.

"Seven minutes and four seconds,"
Mr. Quinty says.

I put my hands behind my head and
walk to catch my breath.

"Elgin, great job," Mr. Quinty
says. "You've improved more than
anyone else out here."

I didn't break seven minutes. But his words mean a lot to me.

HOME. I run up the stairs, unlock the front door, and step inside.

"Hi, Mom!"

No answer. Today was her day off. I get a bad feeling.

I look in the living room. It's empty. The kitchen is empty, too.

I look in her bedroom. She's sleeping on top of the bed with her mouth open. There's an empty vodka bottle on the floor.

She moves when I shake her. But she doesn't wake up.

I sit on the floor next to her bed and hang my head.

She went four months without drinking.

It's happening again.

AFTER DINNER. Mom is still sleeping. I hear snoring from her room.

I try to do my math homework. But her snoring gets louder.

I can't think.

I try to study for my science test. Her snoring gets quieter.

I still can't think.

I have to get my work done.

But I can't stop worrying about Mom.

16 NEVER BEEN

SUNDAY AFTERNOON. I sit at the top of the stairs outside our apartment.

Dad is late. And he didn't pay the child support again. But I don't have to worry about Mom coming out to start something.

She was drinking and fell asleep an hour ago.

Ten minutes pass. Dad pulls up. There's no reason to hurry.

I walk down the stairs and get in his car.

DAD'S PLACE. We park and go up the stairs to his apartment. He seems like he's in a hurry.

Francine gives me one of her hugs. We go to the living room.

I should have known. It's racing season. Dad turns on the Pennzoil 400.

Francine sits next to Dad on the couch. I sit by myself in the side chair.

"Who are you betting on?" Francine asks Dad.

He opens his laptop and types into his gambling site. "Ricky Weatherby and Darnell Jarrett."

I watch Dad's eyes. They stay glued to the race. A commercial comes on.

"Elgin, how are things at school?" he asks me.

"Pretty good. I got a B on my history test."

"Not bad," he says. "How's track?"

"We have a meet on Thursday against Franklin."

"Good," he says. "Maybe I can be there."

I knew he would say that.

But he's never been to a track meet yet.

He doesn't even know what event I run.

The car race goes on. Dad looks at the TV and nothing else. It's the same with Francine.

I'm sitting in the same room with them. But the reality is that I'm all alone.

I get up, leave a note on the kitchen table to say that I went home, and walk out the front door.

I wonder when they'll notice I'm gone. I turn down the sidewalk and don't look back.

HOME. I unlock the front door. I hope it's not going to be bad.

But it is.

Mom sleeps in the easy chair with her mouth wide open.

There's a splotch of blood on the front of her T-shirt.

She coughs. Blood drips from the corner of her mouth.

I shake her shoulder. She sleeps. I shake it again. She sleeps on.

I sit on the couch where I can watch her.

Ten minutes pass.

She opens her eyes, stands up, and staggers to her bedroom.

She doesn't see me. She doesn't
know I'm here.

EVENING. Mom and I sit at the
kitchen table. I made cheese
macaroni and salad for dinner.

"Feeling any better?" I ask.

"A little," she says. "I don't
know why I'm so tired."

The whites of her eyes are
yellow. Her skin is gray.

I'll be glad when she sees the
doctor on Wednesday.

She's never been this bad before.

17 ALL ALONE

TRACK PRACTICE. We sit on the grass and stretch. Mr. Quinty stands in front of us.

"Make sure your parents come for open house tonight," he says. "I want them to talk with all of your teachers."

I'm glad Mom is coming. She's working today, so she won't be drunk. The teachers are going to say nice things about me.

"And make sure you get to bed early tonight," Mr. Quinty says. "We have a good chance to beat Franklin tomorrow."

I'll be running the 1600 meters. I won't be fast enough to score any points. But I think I can break seven minutes.

HOME. I unlock the front door and step inside.

Open house starts in thirty minutes.

"Mom, are you ready?"

No answer.

The living room is empty. There's coughing from her bedroom.

I look through her door. Her sheets are covered in blood.

Every time she coughs, blood spurts out of her mouth.

I rush to the bed and lift her head up.

She looks at me. I see fear in her eyes.

She squeezes my hand. I pull her close to me.

She coughs again.

Blood comes out.

I call 911.

"Help! My mom! She's bleeding!"

HOSPITAL. I look around the waiting room. I've been here for two hours.

There's nothing new to see.

I look at my scrubs. The hospital gave them to me because my clothes were soaked with blood.

Mom's blood.

A lady in a blue sweater smiles at me. She seems nice.

I can't smile back.

Another hour passes.

A woman who looks like a doctor

comes through the double doors.

"Are you Elgin?" she asks.

I follow her to an area where there are fewer people. I wish I had somebody with me.

"Your mom is doing better," the doctor says. "The bleeding and coughing have stopped."

"What happened?" I ask.

"Does your mom drink alcohol?"

"Sometimes."

"Very much?"

"Yes."

"It could be liver damage, possibly cirrhosis," the doctor says. "It can happen with heavy alcohol use. That's what might be causing the bleeding."

"Will my mom get better?"

The doctor's eyes turn away. "She's stable now and sleeping. You can see her in a little while."

The doctor turns and goes back through the double doors.

I go back to my seat.

She didn't answer my question. I know what that means.

I look at the floor. Tears start.

The lady in the blue sweater gets up and sits next to me

She pulls me close.

I can't stop crying.

She pulls me closer.

I'm all alone.

18 NOT GOOD

WEDNESDAY MORNING. I sit in Mom's hospital room. The sun comes up and shines through the window.

Her eyes open. I'm glad to see her smile. But the whites of her eyes are yellow.

It's because of the cirrhosis. I read about it on my phone while I watched her sleep last night.

"Elgin, thanks for staying with me," she says. "But it's time for you to get out of here."

"What do you mean?"

"I want you to go home, get changed, and go to school," she says. "And I want you running in the track meet today."

"I thought it would be good if I stayed here with you."

"No, it wouldn't," she says. "I want you in school."

I move to the bed and hug her.

I don't want to let her go.

HISTORY CLASS. It's hard to stay awake. I'm still tired from last night.

I sit up straight and open my eyes wide. We're writing essays. I don't want to fall asleep.

Mr. Rubio kneels next to me. "Elgin, I missed seeing your mom last night," he says.

"Something came up," I say. "She

wasn't feeling good."

I wish I could tell him what really happened. But I can't do it here.

Ten minutes pass. My cell phone vibrates. I keep it under my desk and check it. It's a text from Mom.

Saw doctor. Coming home tomorrow. Run hard.

I don't feel like running today. I would rather be with Mom.

TRACK MEET. We line up for the 1600 meters. I want to break seven minutes. I wish I felt better.

I look into the bleachers again. Dad isn't there. I didn't think he would be.

The official raises the starting

pistol. Bang!

I round the first turn.

My breathing is hard. My legs and arms feel heavy.

I see Mom in my mind. She's coughing up blood.

All I could do was hold her head up and wait for the paramedics to get there. It took forever.

Second lap. I remember the emergency room. People were yelling at me, asking questions about Mom.

I was scared she was going to die.

Third lap. I remember the look on the doctor's face. She didn't want to tell me how bad Mom was.

Final lap. My lungs burn. My legs are dead. I cross the finish line.

"Seven minutes and thirty-one seconds," the official says.

I'm glad the race is over.

I don't care about the time.

HOSPITAL. I get off the elevator.
Mom told me to stay home. But I have
to see her.

She's sleeping when I get to her
room. She looks peaceful, like she's
having a good dream.

I kiss her forehead and sit in
the chair next to her.

She turns and opens her eyes. I'm
glad to see her smile.

HOME. I finish washing Mom's sheets
and blankets. I also dump the last
of her vodka down the sink.

Everything is ready for her to
come home tomorrow.

I'm tired. I need to sleep. But I
have to do homework.

In math, I do everything for yesterday and today. I also do the Khan Academy.

In science, we have a test tomorrow on outer space. I skim the chapter, answer the questions in the study guide, and read my notes again.

For art, I draw a picture of Mom smiling. It feels good to look at it, to think of her that way.

I remember how I felt when I rode with Mom to the hospital.

Blood was everywhere. I squeezed her hand. I wanted the ambulance to go faster.

Mom looked better tonight. But I know what's going to happen.

There's no cure for cirrhosis of the liver.

She's going to get worse.

19 IF I HAVE TO

THURSDAY MORNING. MATH. I begin the
warm-up assignment.

Mr. Braden walks around the
classroom. He hands back our tests
from yesterday.

I get a B.

Mom comes home from the hospital
this afternoon.

It will be nice to show her.

HOME. I run up the stairs. I can't
wait to see Mom.

I step inside.

The smell hits me.

Alcohol.

Mom sits at the kitchen table with her coffee cup. It probably has vodka in it.

"Hi honey!" she says. "How was school?"

It makes me mad that she's smiling.

The more she drinks, the less time she's going to have.

She'll be gone.

EVENING. The house is quiet. My homework is done.

I open the door to Mom's bedroom. She's sound asleep.

I look in her closet. There's a bottle of vodka in her jacket.

I look in her dresser. I find another bottle.

I check the rest of her room. Nothing.

She must have had the rideshare driver stop at a liquor store on the way home from the hospital.

I leave Mom's room and dump out the vodka in the kitchen sink.

It feels good to watch it go down the drain.

I put the empty bottles on the table for her to see in the morning.

I'll do it every night if I have to.

20 PROUD OF ME

FRIDAY MORNING. SCIENCE. Ms. Acosta starts class.

The door opens. It's a blue slip for me to see the principal.

Why would he send for me?

I get to the office. Dr. Vinson comes from behind his desk and shakes my hand.

It surprises me to see him smile. He's always serious when I see him around campus.

"Elgin, I called you in so I could congratulate you," he says.

"You made the honor roll."

I take a breath. Nothing like this has ever happened to me before.

"I looked at your records," he says. "I know you were struggling when the school year started. I'm proud of you."

He gives me a certificate. I read the words.

Edison High School. Elgin Hobbs. You are hereby named to the Principal's Honor Roll for earning outstanding grades on the fifteen-week report card. Congratulations on your fine achievement.

I feel good inside. I've never received an award during all my years in school.

HISTORY. We're writing essays about democracy. I'm almost done.

Mr. Rubio kneels next to me. "Elgin, I recommended you to be a peer counselor," he says. "They need new people. I said you would be outstanding."

"What do I do?"

"From time to time, they will ask you to speak to other students. You will tell them about your experiences and what you did to improve."

"Why did you pick me?"

"You've made it through some tough times this year. I think you can help other students who are having problems."

I don't know what to say. I've never been picked for anything before.

EVENING. Mom and I cook pancakes and bacon for dinner.

She's sober tonight. It feels good to stand next to her.

I think about my honor roll certificate.

She cried when she saw it. Then, I started crying.

I look at Mom again. I know she's not going to get better.

But I'm going to keep working hard. I'm going to keep doing my best.

She'll be proud of me.

ACKNOWLEDGMENTS

I would like to express my sincere gratitude to all of the people who gave me feedback while I was writing this book.

COFFEE HOUSE WRITERS GROUP:
Christine Marie Bryant, Bahni Byrd, Nicholas Chiazza, Anuarite Chizungu, Robyn Dolan, Synida Fontes, Clyde Fugami, Sabrina Graham, Kevin Hill, Helene Hoffman, J. Bryan Jones, Alex Khansa, Brandon Kuys, John Lowell, Taylor Mari, Dollie Mason, Mark Mason, Scott McClelland, Dav Pauli, Jean Pliska, Erigena Sallaku, Shannon Schermerhorn, Lorraine Silvers, Sara Skinner, Tom Wagner, Emily Wilder, AnneLise Wilhelmson, and Dennis Wolverton.

SOCIETY OF CHILDREN'S BOOK WRITERS AND ILLUSTRATORS: Tim Burke, Christine Carter, Jonathan Chew, Mandy Chew, Byron Go, Lisa Gold, Chuck Grieb, Jamie Hamilton, Emily Heebner, Christine Henderson, Carrie Honigman, Niki House, Christine Jelbert, Jan Larratt-Smith, Chris Powers, Kelly Powers, Jodi Rizzotto, Esther Tenenbaum, Kathleen Troy, Teri Vitters, and Eric Young.

Thank you, Pam Sheppard, for your advice on creating this series.

Thank you, Laura Perkins, for your careful editing and guidance.

Thank you, Betty-Jean, for your patience, your suggestions, and for being my wife.

ABOUT THE AUTHOR

 My dream of becoming a writer started at Whitworth University. I was lucky to have a teacher, Dr. Tammy Reid, who believed in me and encouraged me. After college, I began a career as an educator, teaching reading and English at a middle school in Los Angeles. I went to college at night to earn a doctorate in education. I then served as a high-school principal and district administrator. One of the most important things I have learned is that everyone can achieve success. Set your sights high, work hard, and never give up. Strive to be the best that you can be.

FINDING FORWARD BOOKS

At Finding Forward Books, we publish easy-to-read novels about real issues that show teens overcoming challenges in their lives. Our goal is to help students improve their reading skills, increase their success in school, and develop positive attitudes.

The books are suitable for all students, including English learners and those with learning disabilities. Lexile measures range from 390 to 560.

They have been praised in *Kirkus Reviews*, *Publishers Weekly BookLife Reviews*, *Foreword Clarion Reviews*, and *BlueInk Reviews*.

ADDITIONAL TITLES

TAKEN AWAY. A teen learns to cope after his dad is sent to prison.

NO PLACE TO HIDE. A discouraged student improves his reading skills.

NEVER WANTED. A neglected teen is placed in a foster home.

KNOCKED DOWN. A football player learns the importance of honesty.

TORN. A student with everything learns to care about a student who has nothing.

OVERSPRAY. A teen experiences grief after his father dies.

BLUE WALL. A troubled teen battles back from depression.

LETTERZ. A teen struggling with dyslexia learns how to succeed in school.

CANS. A teen who dreams of attending college struggles against poverty

FINDING HOME. A homeless teen struggles to find a better life.

Finding Forward Books
Easy-to-Read Novels About Real
Issues Faced by Teens
www.findingforwardbooks.com